This Little Tiger book belongs to:

_____

_____

_____

To the Stüllenberg family, Birgit,
Holger, Ricarda and Sabrina
(not forgetting Honey!), with love always x
~ C F

For Norinda
~ V V

LITTLE TIGER PRESS LTD,
an imprint of the Little Tiger Group
1 Coda Studios, 189 Munster Road,
London SW6 6AW
www.littletiger.co.uk

First published in Great Britain 2012
This edition published 2016

ISBN 978-1-84869-455-2
Printed in China
LTP/2700/2736/0319

4 6 8 10 9 7 5 3

The Sleepy Way Home to Bed

Claire Freedman

Veronica Vasylenko

LITTLE TIGER
LONDON

The sun was glowing gold, and the trees cast
long shadows in the soft dappled light.
"Home time, Little Hare!" called Mummy Hare.
"It's nearly bedtime!"
"But Mummy, I'm not tired!" cried Little Hare.

"Well," said Mummy. "Let's walk the sleepy way back home."

"What's the sleepy way home?" asked Little Hare.

"You'll soon see," Mummy smiled.

Mummy and Little Hare
skippity-skipped across the
babbling brook, as Mouse
scampered by.

"Hello, Mouse!" said Little Hare excitedly.

"We're walking the sleepy way home tonight," Mummy Hare told Mouse with a wink. "It's to help a hoppity little hare fall fast asleep!"

"Oh, I see!" smiled Mouse with a twinkle in his eye. "I know that special path. Follow me, Little Hare!"

Giggling, Little Hare went scurrying and hurrying after Mouse.

At last, puffing and panting, Mouse
flopped on the soft grass. Mummy
Hare laughed.

"You must be tired out too, Little Hare?"

"Not me!" Little Hare giggled.

Further along the path, Little Hare
saw Little Bunny and his mummy.
"Hello, Little Bunny," said Little Hare.
"Mummy's taking me the sleepy way home
tonight – it's fun!"

"But Little Hare's bouncier than ever!" sighed Mummy Hare.

Mummy Rabbit smiled.

"It always helps to have a nice full tummy before bedtime," she said. "Especially if the berries are picked from this special sleepy-time bush!"

"Ooooh!" cried Little Hare in wonder.

"Please can I try one, Mummy?"

"Of course!" Mummy Hare nodded.

So Little Hare and Little Bunny munched happily.

Soon, Little Bunny was yawning, but Little Hare was still full of bounce.

As Little Hare and Mummy reached
the meadow, they met Horse.

"Guess what, Horse?" Little Hare smiled.

"We're walking the sleepy way home!"

"When *I* walk the sleepy way home,

I often stop for a bedtime story!" said Horse.

"Please can *I* hear one?" Little Hare cried.

They cuddled up cosily and listened to Horse's
sleepy-time story.

"Wasn't that lovely?" sighed Mummy. "You're
looking a tiny bit sleepy, Little Hare!"

"Not even a teeny-weeny bit!" Little Hare yawned.

As Little Hare
skipped ahead, Owl
swooped down from
the star-studded sky.
"I hear that you're
walking the sleepy way
home tonight," called Owl.
"This is my sleepy lullaby tree!
Would you like a lullaby?"
"Oh, please!" cried Little Hare.
"Tu-whit, tu-whoo! Sweet dreams to you!" Owl sang softly.
"Tu-whit, tu-whoo . . ." sang Little Hare, rubbing his eyes.

Gently, Mummy took
Little Hare's paw. They
counted the twinkling stars and
waved to the sleepy moon, shining
silvery bright in the sky.

"Are you sleepy yet, Little Hare?" Mummy whispered,
as they reached their cosy home at last.

Little Hare nodded drowsily.

"It's working, Mummy!" he said. "Can we walk the
sleepy way back home again tomorrow?"

"Of course," smiled Mummy Hare.
She kissed his little furry ears and his little
furry nose, and gave him a big hare hug.
But Little Hare was already fast asleep!